Yellow Dress Day

Michelle Worthington
illustrated by
Sophie Norsa

Sandy Creek
NEW YORK

Ava loved dresses.

She had a dress in every
color of the rainbow.

Welcome....

Ava's
House

Every morning, Ava jumped out
of bed, ran to the window,
and looked outside.

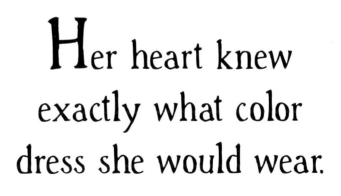

Her heart knew
exactly what color
dress she would wear.

On red dress days
the sun shines on
cracked, dry
roads and Ava's puppy
lies panting in the shade
of the big tree.

On pink dress days
flowers open their
petals toward the sun and

busy bees buzz
and hum

around Ava's garden.

On purple dress days the
rumble tumble
clouds grumble in the sky
and the big fat drops of
rain tap at Ava's window.

On blue dress days
snowflakes
swish
and swirl
and fall

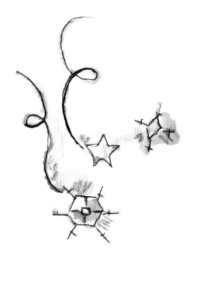

like sparkles from
the sky to make
Ava's nose twitch
with the cold.

On yellow dress days
the whistling
wind ruffles Ava's hair
and tugs at the leaves
on the trees, making
the branches

shiver and shake.

One whistling, whirly, windy day,

Ava looked for her yellow dress.

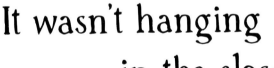

It wasn't hanging in the closet.

It wasn't folded in the drawer.

It wasn't crumpled under her bed.

Ava remembered that yesterday had also been a whistling, whirly, windy day.

She had worn her yellow dress
as she jumped
and tumbled
in a big pile of leaves.

She finally found her yellow dress
in the laundry hamper.

Ava's heart sank.

Mommy found an old box full of dressing-up clothes.

On a yellow dress day, could Ava be a

firefighter?

A daffodil?

A ballerina?

Ava put on the
yellow daffodil costume
and went outside
to play.

The whistling wind tugged at Ava's hair as she whirled around and around in the sunshine.

It was the best
yellow dress day
ever.

For Ava Larder. MW

For all the Norsas,
including Winnie, my cat. SN

IRSF
INTERNATIONAL
RETT SYNDROME
FOUNDATION

Rett syndrome strikes all racial and ethnic groups, and occurs worldwide in 1 of every 10,000 to 23,000 female births. It is a developmental disorder that causes problems in brain function that are responsible for cognitive, sensory, emotional, motor, and autonomic function. Part of the proceeds from the sale of this book go directly to the International Rett Syndrome Foundation on behalf of Ava Larder.

Sandy Creek
NEW YORK

An Imprint of Sterling Publishing
387 Park Avenue South
New York, NY 10016

This 2013 edition published by Sandy Creek, by arrangement with New Frontier Publishing.

Designed by Celeste Hulme

ISBN 978-1-4351-4922-9

Manufactured in Hong Kong, China
Lot #:
2 4 6 8 10 9 7 5 3 1
06/13